W
MW00975119
R
Q
P
M
L
K
G
F
C
B
A

 Published in the United States by Random House Children's Books, a division of Penguin Random House LLC, 1745 Broadway, New York, NY 10019, and in Canada by Penguin Random House Canada Limited, Toronto, in conjunction with Disney Enterprises, Inc. Random House and the colophon are registered trademarks of Penguin Random House LLC.
randomhousekids.com
ISBN 978-0-7364-3818-6
Printed in China
10 9 8 7 6 5 4 3

Disney · PIXAR
Cars

Mater's Backward ABC Book

A to Z?
No!
Z to A.

Let's begin at the end.

Try it my way!

By Lisa Wheeler

Illustrated by Satoshi Hashimoto

Random House New York

Zigzag!

It's the letter Z.

I'm **Z**ooming and **Z**ipping!

***Z**ap!*

Follow me!

Yippee! It's the letter **Y**.

Yield on **y**ellow . . .

Yee-haw!

Goodbye!

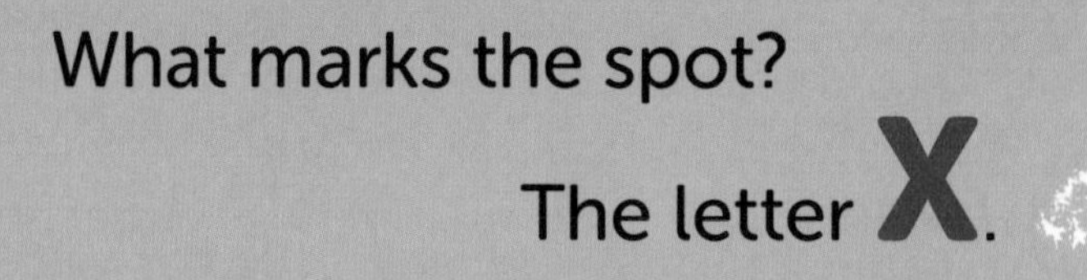

What marks the spot?

The letter **X**.

A railroad crossing!

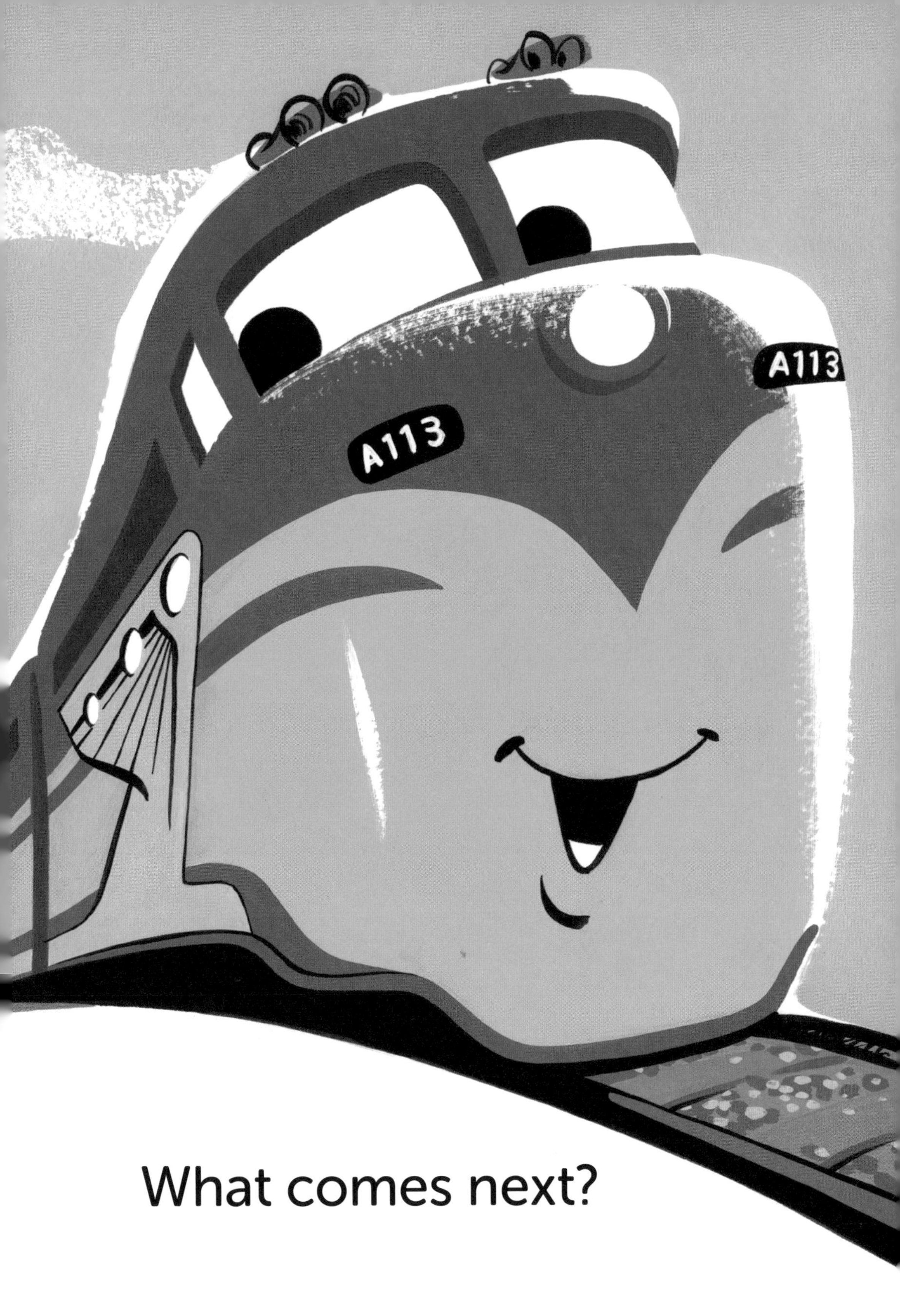

What comes next?

*W*hooo-wheee! It's a **W**.

My **W**heels are **W**hirring round.

McQueen **w**ins at **W**illys Butte,

but I just kick up ground.

V is for ***V**room! **V**room!*

Out of the way!

I **v**eer to a stop

at the **V**8 Café.

Ultra and **u**nleaded gas

both begin with **U**.

Uh-oh. I'm nearly empty!

I need a gallon or two!

T is for **t**ruck
and the "**T**ow" in **T**ow Mater.
My **t**aillights and **t**rusty hook
wave "See ya later!"

"Surprise!"

It's the letter **S**.

A party is in full swing.

Someone special is

surrounded by friends

while Sarge and Sally sing.

95

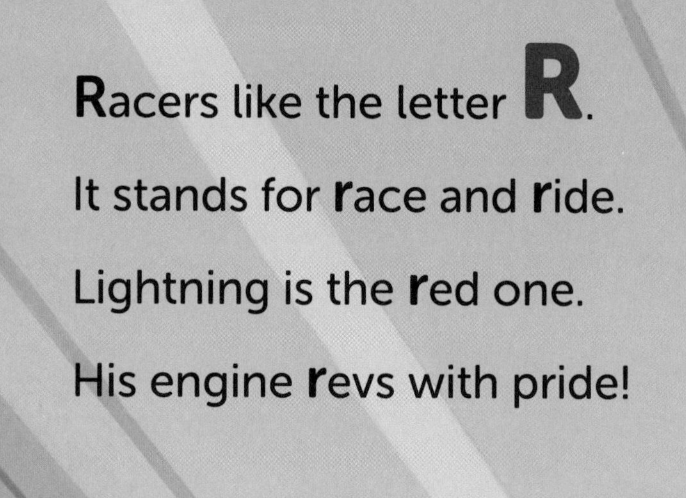

Racers like the letter **R**.

It stands for **r**ace and **r**ide.

Lightning is the **r**ed one.

His engine **r**evs with pride!

Here's the letter **Q**.

What does Lightning say?

"Faster than fast. **Q**uicker than **q**uick."

That's how he wins each day!

P is for the **p**urple **p**aint
Ramone **p**ours in his **p**ail.
He **p**aints a **p**erfect **p**instripe
on a **p**ickup, front to tail!

O is for **O**dometer.

Lizzie sure is bold!

She's turned **O**ver a lot of miles.

You'd never guess she's **O**ld!

95
Kingman
San Bernardino
California

The **n**icest words that start with **N**

are **n**eon and **n**avigation,

nuts and bolts and **n**ighty-**n**ight

and **n**eighbors at the station!

RADIATOR SPRINGS

M is for **M**ater. Hey, that's **m**e!

My **m**uffler's covered in crud.

Mack and **m**e got **m**essy

motoring through the **m**ud.

Rust·eze

L is for **L**ightning

and the **L**egends.

They **l**ove to take a **l**ap.

Around they go! They **l**oop the track.

They'll never need a map!

MASVILLE

Next up is the letter **K**.

The **K**ing is one of a **k**ind!

The fans collect his **k**eepsakes,

and every one is signed.

Jackson Storm starts with a **J**.

With a juiced-up engine, he zooms by.

See his jet-black paint and jeering face.

Just sit back and watch him fly!

I is for **i**dling in low gear
in lots of **i**ce and snow.
I drive along the roadside
in search of cars to tow.

H is for the **h**ighway.
A **h**opped-up **h**ot rod's stuck!
Hooray! I am a **h**ero—
a **h**elpful **h**auling truck!

G is for **g**ears and **g**auges,
gearboxes, **g**askets, and **g**rille **g**uards.
All these **g**oods are worth more than **g**old
and can be found in my **g**rimy junkyard!

Friend begins with the letter **F**,

and it **f**its for **F**illmore and **F**lo.

They make and sell **f**antastic **f**uel.

Fill 'er up and go!

Flo's
V8

E is for **e**ngine!

Each car has a heart.

Gas or **e**lectric,

it's there from the start.

ENGINE

D means **d**ozens of **d**amaging **d**ents.

Does **d**riving get any stranger?

It's **d**emolition **d**erby time.

Watch out—they're **d**odging **d**anger!

The Crazy Eight begins with C.

Crunched cars crash and collide.

Cruz is caught in this race.

Can she find a place to hide?

B is for **b**rakes. **B**oy, oh, **b**oy!

Barreling down a **b**umpy ridge

I **b**op and **b**umble **b**ackward. . . .

Whoa!

Stop!

There ain't no **b**ridge!

We **a**bsolutely end with **A**.

What an **a**mazing ride!

My **a**xles **a**che, but I'm **a**wake,

and friends **a**re by my side.

Z to **A**

or

A to **Z**.

I'm glad you spent some time with me.

We had such fun! Is this the end?

Let's go to **Z** and start again!

A B C

F G H

L M

P Q R

V W